TO: ....

FROM: ....

ON THE
OCCASION OF: ....

DATE: ....

SNOWED UNDER

and Other Christmas Confusions

by Serge Bloch

STERLING CHILDREN'S BOOKS
New York

STERLING CHILDREN'S BOOKS
New York

An Imprint of Sterling Publishing
387 Park Avenue South
New York, NY 10016

STERLING CHILDREN'S BOOKS and the distinctive Sterling Children's Books logo are trademarks of Sterling Publishing Co., Inc.

Text © 2011 by Sterling Publishing Co., Inc. Illustrations © 2011 by Serge Bloch. *Designed by Katrina Damkoehler*

The artwork for this book was created using pen and ink drawings with photography.

ISBN 978-1-4027-7131-6 (HC-PLC with Jacket)

Library of Congress Cataloging-in-Publication Data
Bloch, Serge.
  Snowed under and other Christmas confusions / by Serge Bloch.
    p. cm.
  Summary: A snow storm the day before Christmas causes a boy many worries, which are not helped by such confusing phrases as "Don't be a wet blanket" and "That's the way the cookie crumbles."
  ISBN 978-1-4027-7131-6 (hc-plc with jacket : alk. paper) [1. Figures of speech--Fiction. 2. Christmas-- Fiction. 3. Humorous stories.] I. Title.
  PZ7.B61943Sn 2011
  [E]--dc22
                                        2010037056

Distributed in Canada by Sterling Publishing
c/o Canadian Manda Group, 165 Dufferin Street
Toronto, Ontario, Canada M6K 3H6
Distributed in the United Kingdom by GMC Distribution Services
Castle Place, 166 High Street, Lewes, East Sussex, England BN7 1XU
Distributed in Australia by Capricorn Link (Australia) Pty. Ltd.
P.O. Box 704, Windsor, NSW 2756, Australia

For information about custom editions, special sales, and premium and corporate purchases,
please contact Sterling Special Sales at 800-805-5489 or specialsales@sterlingpublishing.com.

Manufactured in China
Lot #:
2 4 6 8 10 9 7 5 3 1
06/11

It was the day before Christmas,
and the snow had just started to fall.
"Out of bed, sleepyhead!" called my mother.
"We're going to have to **work our tails off**
to get ready for Christmas tomorrow."

Dad was in the kitchen listening to the radio.
I heard the weatherman say that
a giant snowstorm was brewing for Christmas Eve.

As we were eating breakfast, I told Dad
my Christmas wish list. My sister said,
"Don't count your chickens before they hatch."

"Tonight's storm is going to be SO BIG that Santa will probably **get stuck** at the North Pole," she whispered.

Dad told her not to be such a **wet blanket.**

"Where's your **Christmas spirit?**" he asked her.

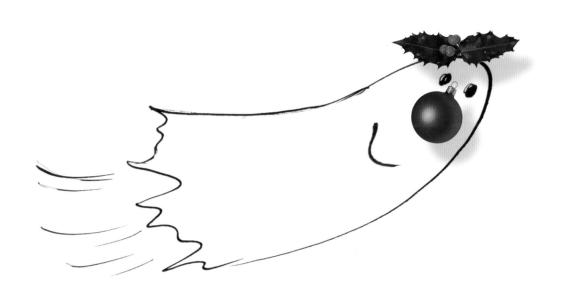

I was pretty sure Santa would know exactly what to do in bad weather.
Just to be safe, I decided to ask Grandpa.
He told me that my sister was just trying to **get my goat**.

Then he said, "Santa will miss Christmas **when pigs fly!**"

His advice was very confusing, and I was starting to feel nervous.
"What's wrong?" asked Grandma.
"Looks like someone **took the wind right out of your sails.**"

When I told her about Santa and the snowstorm, she said not to worry.
"Santa is **king of the hill** when it comes to winter travel."

She suggested that I get my mind off of my troubles
by helping her **trim the tree**...

...and **deck the halls.**

Then my mother asked me to help her peel potatoes because we were going to be **feeding an army** on Christmas Day.

When I told her how worried I was about Santa,
she said that he wasn't the *only* one who felt **snowed under**...

...and **tied up in knots.**

"Your dad and I got up at the **crack of dawn**...

...and have been running around like **hamsters in a wheel** ever since!" she said.

After lunch, Dad asked us to clean our room,
since our cousins would all be spending the night with us.
"We're going to be **packed in like sardines**," grumbled my sister.

"You'll be **snug as a bug in a rug!**" said my dad with a wink.

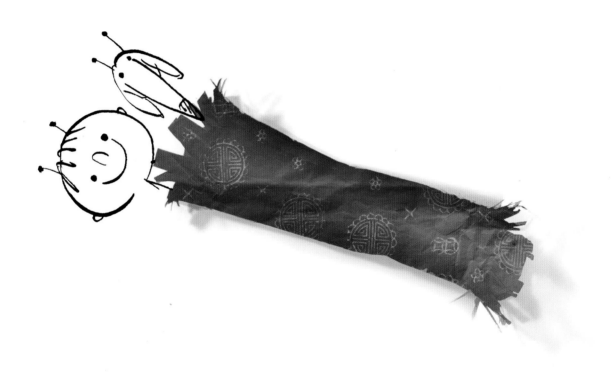

Then he told us not to miss **the big picture.**
"**Birds of a feather flock together,**" he said.
"And being together is what Christmas is all about."

But it seemed like Christmas would *never* come.
Grandpa said he knew just how I felt.
"Time moves at a snail's pace
when you're waiting for something..."

"...but **time flies** when you're having **fun!**"
Grandpa challenged me and Roger to a snowball fight.
We *definitely* won.

When we went inside to get warm,
the kitchen smelled like cinnamon and baked apples.
Grandpa said he was **as hungry as a bear**!

After dinner, we sang Christmas carols.
Grandma said she was proud of me for finding a way
to be more **light-hearted**.

That night, Dad tucked my sister and me into bed.
Outside our window, the snowdrifts were as tall as our fence.
"You don't need to worry," Dad said to me.
"Santa will **go to the ends of the Earth** to find you."

After Dad turned out the light, my sister said,
"If Santa can't get here tonight,
that's just the way the cookie crumbles!"

Cookies! I'd forgotten all about leaving Santa some.
I sneaked into the kitchen to make Santa a snack.
"Aha! Caught you **red-handed!**" said my mother.

When I told her what I was doing, she said I was **an angel** and helped me pour a glass of milk for Santa.

Grandpa said that getting us to bed on Christmas Eve
was like **pulling teeth**. I *finally* fell asleep.
When I woke up the next morning and saw that
Santa had come after all . . .

...I lit up like a Christmas tree!